Buster

PRAISE FOR *STORYSHARES*

"One of the brightest innovators and game-changers in the education industry."
– Forbes

"Your success in applying research-validated practices to promote literacy serves as a valuable model for other organizations seeking to create evidence-based literacy programs."

- Library of Congress

"We need powerful social and educational innovation, and Storyshares is breaking new ground. The organization addresses critical problems facing our students and teachers. I am excited about the strategies it brings to the collective work of making sure every student has an equal chance in life."
– Teach For America

"Around the world, this is one of the up-and-coming trailblazers changing the landscape of literacy and education."
- International Literacy Association

"It's the perfect idea. There's really nothing like this. I mean wow, this will be a wonderful experience for young people."   - Andrea Davis Pinkney, Executive Director, Scholastic

"Reading for meaning opens opportunities for a lifetime of learning. Providing emerging readers with engaging texts that are designed to offer both challenges and support for each individual will improve their lives for years to come. Storyshares is a wonderful start."
- David Rose, Co-founder of CAST & UDL

Buster

Darryl Armstrong

STORYSHARES

Story Share, Inc.
New York. Boston. Philadelphia

Published in the United States by Story Share, Inc.

Storyshares
Story Share, Inc.
24 N. Bryn Mawr Avenue #340
Bryn Mawr, PA 19010-3304
www.storyshares.org

Inspiring reading with a new kind of book.

Interest Level: Middle School
Grade Level Equivalent: 4.9

9781642616033

Book design by Storyshares

Printed in the United States of America

Storyshares Presents

Prologue

In the 1920s and 30s, a "buster" was a word used to describe difficult children. My friend, Gurney Howard, was nicknamed Buster. This name stuck with him until his death. I have often wondered if I should send a note to God and ask him how much things have changed since he brought Buster up there. If Buster made it there. Maybe the Devil thought Buster belonged to him. But I think God investigated Buster's heart and brought him home.

I just laugh when I remember this unusual kid from my childhood. His endless supply of antics could not all be listed one place. However, there are enough for you to understand what it was like to grow up with a friend like Buster.

2

Buster's mother, Frances, pointed a finger in his face. "You are not to touch that bow and arrow inside this house, young man. Do you understand me?"

"Yes, ma'am," Buster's said as he dropped his birthday present. He had already shot a couple arrows out the back window. He knew that being caught was unwise.

Frances felt sorry for her highly energetic son. "I know you have been penned up here for more than a week with all this rain. But even if you go out it's probably flooded. I'm worn out trying to think of stuff for you to do. Why don't you go read a book?"

The next morning, the weather cleared. Buster raced outside as soon as he washed his breakfast dishes.

As he passed my house, Buster gave the secret whistle. It sounded like a weird bird call. I rushed out with half of my breakfast in a napkin.

We met up with one of the Chambers twins, Rufe, the one Buster liked. All three of us walked together. We were glad to be away from adults and exploring the rain-soaked area. Buster always turned an ordinary day in the Michigan woods into a Lewis and Clark journey.

"Let's go down by the creek." Buster motioned toward the normally slow-moving creek, which looped around the farming community. "Gotta be some pretty high water by now. Dad said that Miller's Dairy flooded and his cows got stranded. Let's go see."

The three of us half-walked and half-ran down to the creek. Wooden fence posts were still damp and dripping. Ditches lined the lane, filled with rainwater.

Climbing over Miller's pasture gate had been standard practice for us farming kids. We had to get to the creek somehow. Usually Ol' Snort, Miller's breeding bull, stood between us and the creek. But today he must have been on the other side of the pasture due to the high water. The three of us sloshed our way to the back fence. We climbed over it expertly and continued toward the creek.

A long line of debris showed how high the water was. Six feet higher than the normal mark. Water moved swiftly down the usually calm creek. We walked to the free-range area of the pasture, side-stepping as much of the debris as we could. The high water had washed stuff down from miles away. A broken sign from the market selling ears of corn now just read "ears 10 cents." It made us laugh from its place among broken branches, bottles, a used toilet seat, and an old chair.

In the lead, Buster motioned up the trail. "Let's go to the swimmin' hole. Gotta be deep right about now."

The most poorly-kept secret in the county was probably this. All the kids in the area came to swim here, against their parent's permission. On hot summer days we jumped off an overturned stump that housed a family of mink. The kids and the mink had been co-residents for several generations. Swimming in this water, filled with bloodsuckers, meant checking each other for leeches afterwards.

We had learned, years before, to post a lookout

when we used the swimming hole. Miller's cows crossed upstream and dropped what my brother called "Brown Lilies" into the water. Cow patties floated down the stream. You only had seconds to move before they softly collided with you on the surface of the water.

"Careful of this rock, it's wobbly," Buster yelled back to Rufe and me. "After we get around this bend, we'll see if the hole is still there."

"Holy Moses," Rufe and I heard Buster say. We looked up. A big mature black bull had washed to the side of the waterway. He was resting on the bank just before the swimming hole.

"Gawd, look at this, boys. It's one of them black bulls like we see up near Emmet. Big one, too."

"He's dead, ain't he?" Rufe asked.

Buster walked over next to the bull. "Probably not sleeping on his side by the creek, Rufe. Musta drowned and then floated down this way."

We excitedly discussed this incredible find. Then the infamous, inevitable Buster-twist made its appearance. I can't tell you how many weird ideas began with Buster saying, "You know..."

"...I bet we could sell tickets to the other kids just to

see this," Buster said.

Rufe and I looked at Buster with our brows furrowed.

"You know, we could tell 'em that this here bull is the goriest thing they saw. For ten cents we'll lead 'em to it. You *know* the kids will pay for this."

So, we started telling the neighborhood kids about the "awfullest" and "horriblest" thing they will ever see. P.T. Barnum could not have promoted this scene any better than Buster, Rufe, and I did. Buster had a lot of natural sales talent, even as a kid.

"Shhhh, we don't want *everybody* to know," he told some kids. "You just won't believe it! It is the most *fabulous* thing ever to hit Michigan."

The showing date had been scheduled for Sunday, after church. Each kid would have to pay a dime. We assembled at the back of the post office. Word spread through the secret network that only kids knew about.

Ten cents in 1926 equals $1.35 in today's money. Not easy money for a pre-teen kid to lay their hands on. But nobody wanted to be left out of the "most fabulous thing to ever hit Michigan." Lots of piggy banks were turned upside down and shaken.

On Sunday at 1:30, about twelve kids had assembled behind the post office. Buster tried doing the math to figure out how much money we had earned, but multiplication wasn't his strong suit. Plus Buster let Rosie Traufman, the mayor's daughter, in for free. Much to the dismay of the mayor, she was Buster's favorite.

"Stay single file. Remember, when we get to Miller's gate, we gotta watch for Ol' Snort. If he's there, me and Rufe are the fastest. We will lead him to the side pasture while you all make a run for it."

Ol' Snort could not be seen in the pasture. So all of us ran across the field, unchallenged. On bad days when the ferocious bull lurked near the gate, kids would run up a tree half-way across the pasture for safety. Sometimes they would have to wait for hours until Ol' Snort was far enough away to make a run for the fence. The bull could be truly dangerous. But we treated the situation as a necessary evil. We were farm kids.

Buster had his bow and one arrow with him as we climbed through the back fence. "You all stay with me. I will protect us in case somethin' tries to get us."

With the arrow fixed in the twine and the bow slightly flexed, Buster held up "The Equalizer," as he called it. The kids felt confident they were in good, protective hands.

"Now stop here," Buster instructed. "Let me make sure it's still there and ready for viewing."

As he crept around the trees, Buster reached the back of the clearing. He straightened with amazement when he looked at the bull. The summer heat and abdominal gasses had caused it to swell. The bull was now wider than it was long. The drum-like tautness of the belly forced its legs to stick out like a piñata. The sight was even more awful than we promised.

One-by-one, kids in their Sunday finest stepped around the tree and walked over to the carcass. Soon all twelve stood next to the bull. They made gagging sounds as they inspected the bulging eyes, extended tongue, and bloated sides.

Buster stayed back. He didn't want to be near the smelly, fly-covered remains. Buster could have calmly left the area, 36 cents richer after sharing the profits with Rufe and me. He could have called it a success. Instead he aimed an arrow at the dead animal...and released it.

The sharp arrow tip hit the balloon-like belly. An explosion of rotting, maggot-filled flesh shot into the air and rained down on the startled children. Although no real injuries occurred, the gagging children stood in shock. They gaped at each other's clothing, covered in blood and guts.

Rosie's red curls were tangled with dripping pieces of intestines. I had been spared from any real damage because I was standing behind Henry Zeemer, the largest kid in the neighborhood. Rufe took a load of bowel and part of a stomach.

Nine-year-old Buster, last seen running for his home, dropped his bow beside a tree.

Days passed before parents stopped visiting Buster's mother to complain about the disaster to their children's clothes. With each visit, Frances would look at Buster and ask him why he had done such a thing.

In his defense, I know he did not understand his actions until after the event took place.

2

Excuse my language, but it is impossible to describe this event without calling the mayor's outhouse "The Mayor's Shithouse." Even the finest people in town, including Reverend Mills, called it that. In no other context would we have been allowed to use the word "shit."

The mayor owned the bank. He was reelected every four years. His bank held most of the mortgages for homes and business loans in the township. If you owned a business, you sure didn't want to oppose the mayor. Thus, the election results were always the same. Any campaigning was just for show. Phineas T. Traufman would be the mayor if he wanted to be.

Two things are significant at this point. First, the mayor disliked Buster. He took many of Buster's sins to heart. In fact, Buster got his nickname from the mayor.

Years ago, on Arbor Day, the mayor planted a tree and dedicated it to himself. He even put a sign on it to commemorate the event. When Buster was seven years old, the mayor saw Buster peeing on that tree during a campaign event. He started to say, "That little bas—" and quickly changed it to "buster." After all, he was in front of half the town. So, after that, my best friend was known as Buster.

The second fact you must know is about the outhouse itself. It had been designed and built with architectural care. It was not just a corn cob palace like the rest of us had. The walls were made of cement blocks. The outside was done in white clapboard siding to match the house. A functional window had a planter on the inside, with real plants in it.

This structure stood against one side of Main Street. So it was visible to the rest of the town. The mayor showed off his wealth by building this elaborate outhouse. It even had green trim, a metal door, and curtains over the window.

Two days before the mayor's inaugural parade, I went out with Buster. We were patrolling our creek. In early spring, the garter snakes emerged from their winter nap. They were easy to grab as they squirmed lazily along the riverbanks.

"Let's just shove 'em in the sack I brought," said Buster. "I want about a dozen or so."

I did not question his motive for wanting the snakes. It seemed like good sport. We usually grabbed a couple in the spring and took them home as pets.

At dusk, Buster took the sack of snakes over to the mayor's outhouse. He released the serpents into the small structure. After closing the door tightly, he left.

The expected results should have been comical enough, even for Buster. But when the mayor's wife, Florence Traufman, entered the outhouse the next morning...that was more than we had counted on.

Mrs. Traufman went to the outhouse carrying the thunder mugs from the night before. This would normally be a job for their maid, but Mrs. Traufman needed to use the area anyway. So she chose to do the job herself. Upon entering the outhouse, she set the night jars down on the floor. Then she sat down to do her business.

After getting situated, she realized the floor was

writing with snakes. Horrified, she leapt to her feet, tripping over the piss pots. Sliding around on the floor, she managed to open the door. Poor Mrs. Traufman tried to run with her cotton underwear around her ankles, which proved difficult.

The screaming woman was in full view of the early risers on Main Street. Her white thighs scrambled up the lawn, followed by a stream of human waste and snakes. Even though her underwear remained at her ankles, she ran like a penguin for the back door of the house, screeching and swearing the whole way.

The mayor ran downstairs to meet his wife. She was madder than any person he had ever encountered. He could only reach over and meekly hand her a kitchen towel for the side of her dripping arm.

Roy Dixon, the County Sheriff, gathered several of the usual suspects together. He threatened all of us with everything from reform school to death, but nobody ratted out Buster.

The next day, during the inaugural parade, the mayor's float was attacked by fake rubber snakes. No one saw who threw them. The mayor swore that somebody threw a turd, but I am pretty sure it was a brownie. Buster had a good arm.

3

Boys fart. It is a known and accepted fact. Truth is, everybody farts. But the most females do not openly admit to this biological truth.

In the seventh grade locker room, Buster heard one of the boys pass gas. Of course, giggles and admiring applause followed. But Buster couldn't just leave the situation alone. Oh no, he had to address it.

"You know," Buster said in a challenging tone. "I am probably the best farter in the whole school."

Some of the more "mature" boys did not agree with

Buster's remark. Rusty Hecht may have been the most mature of these boys. He had already begun shaving and spoke with a baritone voice. His response caused a hush in the locker room.

"You ain't never let one like me," Rusty said defensively.

And so, Buster bet Rusty a dollar he could out-fart him. They agreed that the match would take place the next day. With the seventh-grade boys as witnesses, they spit in their hands and shook on it.

I leaned back on my locker. I knew that Buster would not only lose but that he probably didn't have a dollar. Then he would have to fight Rusty. I worried about him but what could I do? He had made the choice.

* * *

After class, I caught up with Buster as we left school. "You gotta be crazy to think you can out-fart Rusty. I mean, he's like the missing link. He ain't one of us, Buster. He shaves and probably drinks and everything. Wow, you bet him a dollar. That's a lot of money to lose. "

I stopped and turned to Buster, who had stopped walking. "You know... I have a plan. I can win—easy."

This should have been my cue to find a new friend.

But you must admit that even you, dear reader, are curious to know what this kid could be thinking.

"You know... I been thinkin' about what gives us gas." Buster was on a roll. "I mean, when I eat some of Grampa's pickled pig's feet, or Gramma's sauerkraut and sausage, I bloat up like a beach ball. Add some of the navy beans that Mom's got canned in the pantry and I think I could fill a blimp. Really, this will be an easy dollar for me."

My concerns were eased as I thought about Buster easting cabbage, beans, pickled pig's feet, and whatever else he could find in his kitchen. His grandfather was quite gassy himself. I decided that maybe Buster had genetics on his side.

Gym period was the third class of the day. Buster walked in while all of us were lined up against our lockers. We waited for the Great American Fart Off, as it would later become known around the school.

Rusty seemed confident. He even cranked out a sample out for his team, known as the "Lips That Never Lie Gang." There were a couple of us on Buster's side. But I was the only one who knew that Buster had been eating all kinds of gassy foods since last night.

"Let's move to the shower room," said Rusty.

Buster and Rusty circled each other like gunfighters.

The shower room had been chosen for the acoustics. An impartial committee had been selected. They stood at the ready, prepared to judge.

Rusty's first entry ranked okay by our standards, but it certainly was not a prize winner. His second and third, over the course of thirty minutes, seemed unbeatable. Buster had only been able to give us two in that time. Both were so weak that he hung his head in defeat. He arranged to pay Rusty twenty-five cents per week for the following month.

After school, Buster and I were walking downtown when Buster said, "No idea why the stuff didn't kick in. Usually does. I even ate some herring, raw potato, and drank some of Grampa's barley beer. But nothin'!"

We entered Marston's drug store. With our last couple of nickels we bought a bottle of Coke and sat at the counter. After twenty minutes, Buster straightened upright as his face turned white. He grabbed his lower abdomen.

"Holy cow. I'm gonna explode!"

He rushed into the phone booth about six stools down. I sat there laughing. Nobody knew what he was doing inside the phone booth but me. He held the phone to his mouth and pretended to have a conversation. But frequent telltale sounds of the truth echoed from the enclosure.

Buster's polite attempt to go unnoticed might have worked if Mrs. Traufman hadn't appeared. She walked over to the phonebooth and stood there impatiently, tapping her foot. I fell on the floor laughing when Buster looked at her and then at me with a helpless expression.

Buster continued the fake call. His pleading gaze seemed to say, "*What the hell do I do now?*" I started crying with laughter.

After two polite knocks from Mrs. Traufman, he shrugged his shoulders and exited the booth. He quickly bolted out of the store. Mrs. Traufman stepped in, dropped her packages, and screamed, "Mercy!" She backed out and stood for a moment, realizing that the quality of air in the booth could not sustain life. She gathered her packages and stomped out of the drugstore.

I had barely been able to get a breath between laughs when Sten Svensen walked up behind Mrs. Traufman. He stepped into the phone booth, turned toward the departing Mrs. Traufman, and said, "Damn, woman! What you been eating?"

At the Masonic Lodge, Sten retold the story many times, always beyond the mayor's hearing.

Buster

4

Marking events by school year makes it easier for me to remember when things happened since Buster and I were in the same grade.

Not much happened in this small town. So, Buster became a huge part of my life. His antics kept me occupied. It seemed like he always had a scheme in mine.

That summer, Buster went to the mayor's house every day. He crept through the garden to the window in the den. That's where the maid hung the mynah bird. Each morning the bird could enjoy fresh air and sing to the other birds outside.

For weeks Buster stood under the window sill. He spent nearly an hour each day teaching the bird a new phrase.

The bird was eventually given to a cousin in Indiana after it said, "The mayor is a shithead." It repeated this several times while they waited for the new owners to arrive. The mayor swore it sounded like Buster's voice. But most people felt that his claim was absurd.

* * *

Buster sold apples from the Hallickson's tree, which grew next to their house on County Line Road. The problem was that the Hallickson's did not give Buster permission to take the apples. When the time came for the apple pie fair, Mrs. Hallickson discovered all her apples were gone.

Buster undersold the grocery store by three cents an apple. Nobody could figure out how he could afford to grow and sell them that cheap.

* * *

Herbert Jorgenson had a pond in his yard and filled it with goldfish. There were nearly fifty goldfish in the pond beneath the lily pads.

Buster began netting three to four fish a night. Then he'd sell them for a nickel each to the kids in the neighborhood. He even had a guaranteed replacement policy if the fish died within the first three days.

Business boomed for Buster. He set up his sales using an old apple crate outside the Palace Theater on Moser Street. As the kids left the movie theater, they would see the fish for sale in mason jars. Buster's stock sold out every day in less than twenty minutes.

Mr. Jorgenson finally noticed that his supply of fish was decreasing. He thought racoons were the problem. So he hired a guard to keep the raccoons away from the pond.

Well, he hired Buster to patrol the pond for a couple of nights. Buster reported to Mr. Jogenson that he had seen several 'coons trying to make it to the pond before he shooed them away. After a fence was built around the pond and the fish still disappeared, Mr. Jorgenson finally gave up. He decided the fish were being taken by birds.

* * *

Buster's father worked on the railroad. The summer of 1931, his father offered to give Buster a ride on the train to Washington Township and back. Buster was excited about the opportunity.

Buster's father, Lafayette, toured the train with him

and finally settled him in the caboose for the return trip to home. Buster asked him how he went to the bathroom on the train. In those days, they did not have holding tank bathrooms on trains.

His father explained that, for the most part, "We just stand on the outside of the caboose and water the side of the track. Most of the tracks are out in the countryside anyhow."

It is customary for all of us to watch passing trains. We watch until we see the caboose, which is the last car on the train.

When the urge became strong enough, Buster could not wait to try out this unique way of urination. The slow-moving train chugged through a narrow pass between two dense woods. Buster thought that this would be enough privacy.

Buster stood at the rear of the train. As he let it fly, the trees stopped, opening into a large clearing. The train passed by a church picnic hosted by the honorable P. T. Traufman. By the time Buster realized he was the focal point of one-hundred people at a summer picnic, it was far too late.

Reports of Mayor Traufman throwing rocks after the train were probably exaggerated, but they came from several sources.

* * *

Two days before we started tenth grade, I walked around with Buster. We noticed old Raif Martin abusing his dog, Rex. For all of Buster's shortcomings, he could not ignore animal abuse. Raif was known for his cruelty. This was the last straw for Buster.

Buster picked up small pieces of glass from the bottom of the storage bin behind Handel's grocery store. When bottles were thrown in the trash, some broke as they collided with other items or the walls of the bin. Buster filled an old sock with shards of glass.

That night Buster, crept into Raif's outhouse. He poured a ring of glue around the toilet hole and spread the shards of glass around the seating area. Then he poured salt over the circle for Raif to enjoy the next morning.

Doc Floog said the fiery ring around Raif's rear had to be treated with iodine to prevent infection. When the doc smeared the iodine on, many people who heard the yells from the office said it sounded like the screams of an old hound dog.

Buster

5

Buster rose to my defense during our sophomore year of high school. It was my brother's senior year. We only had one tuxedo in the family. The prom committee had invited me to the Junior-Senior prom. This was a huge honor for me, the kid my brother always treated with such disrespect.

Our one tuxedo posed a problem: who would get to wear the suit? My brother or me? I knew he had become the rightful inheritor, as the eldest. But I really wanted to make my appearance at the prom special debut. Seeing him take the tuxedo frustrated me.

I made the mistake of telling Buster about my misfortune. He rose to the occasion with his famous, "You know..."

"I learned something interesting in chemistry class last week," Buster told me.

That phrase should have been my cue to run in the opposite direction. But I was always intrigued by the way his mind worked. Turns out that a solution of nitrous acid, when combined with urea and ammonia (abundant in human sweat) will make a potent solvent.

However, a diabolical mind like Buster's would not just commit this fact to memory. He wanted to figure out how to apply this chemistry. He decided that the nitrous acid could lie innocently in the seams of a suit. There, it would wait for a catalyst and then turn into a caustic agent.

Three days before the prom, my brother carefully brushed and cleaned the tux. Then he hung it inside his closet. When Buster came to the house, we laid the suit on the bed. Buster swabbed the inside seams with the nitrous acid. Then we hung it on the back of the closet door.

The night of the prom, I arrived early. I had to complete the jobs assigned by the bossy seniors in charge of the prom. Arriving fashionably late, my brother showed up in the now infamous tux. He looked wonderful in the black suit and had a great shine on his shoes. I stood in my passed-down brown suit, harboring thoughts of his early death.

It was the beginning of June. The weather had turned unseasonably warm, making the room hotter than usual. It took only minutes for the dancers to start sweating—my brother included. As he reached up to wave to a friend, I noticed a split in the elbow of the suit. The music became louder and faster. My brother, a great dancer, increased his rhythmic movements.

The suit separated up the back of the coat, exposing the rear of his pants, which also were pulling apart. Soon the pants separated along the inside seams. When his left coat sleeve separated from the shoulder and fell to the dance floor, he stopped, shocked, and began to take inventory of himself. With each movement he continued falling apart in front of the entire school body.

Wrapping his arms around himself, he ducked out the back and headed toward Dad's car.

Students stopped dancing, laughing wildly and they watched him run across the dance floor. Nobody had a clue why this was happening.. No one, that is, except Mr. Jennings, the chemistry teacher.

The following day, I innocently deflected my

brother's accusations. I was so convincing that our father thought my brother was delusional.

I had to be careful not to be alone with him for the next month until he left for the Navy.

6

Being poor in a farming community during the Great Depression did not show as much in our daily lives as it did for folks in cities. We were used to growing our own food. Everyone hunted and fished, canned, preserved, and traded food. We did not have money, but rarely did we go to bed hungry. If the bank would have stayed off our front porch, we may have gotten through the worst ten years in American history with fewer scars.

Unfortunately, my parents, Buster's parents, and most of the community had mortgages to pay. During this time, foreclosures became commonplace. As the bank acquired more and more properties, they began softening their approach.

The county bank had been calling Buster's parents for two weeks. Everybody in town knew about the problem. In small towns there are very few secrets and lies do not last long. Because so many of the people in the county were in the same boat, Frances and Lafayette spoke openly to their friends about their shortages.

"At least I still have my railroad job," Lafayette told his neighbors. "But they have really cut back on my hours. People can't afford to ride the rails right now. Frances still works on and off with the infirmary outside of town. But money is tight because of Pop's illness. Medical bills are high. We are definitely short on money."

Buster and I rarely ate school lunches during this period. Like many other students, we couldn't afford lunch money. So we brought a sandwich or piece of fruit, and that was lunch.

The summers made it easier to eat because the fields around town were filled with ripe vegetables and fruits. We ate everything from apple to corn and potatoes in the woods behind the farms.

Winter was more difficult since crops were dormant and food was scarcer. Lines of men, women, and children from the cities came through our town. But work had not been available for a long time, and locals weren't able to spare extra food or clothing.

During the winter of 1932 I heard the feared, iconic phrase come out of Buster's mouth: "You know… We could help some of the folks who are starving if we got more people around here to share. I mean, look at Miller's dairy. They have extra milk, eggs, and all kinds of food."

Buster had a faraway look in his eye as he spoke. "I've got an idea of how we can get some food for the hungry people who stop by our town.

"We gotta put on a big show in the gym. We can get people to perform for free. Like old Mrs. Kelton, who plays the harmonica. Or Doris Janeway, who can sing and yodel. And gosh, some of us could write a skit and act it out. Maybe Doc Floog will play his banjo. We can get Sten and the boys to sing some barbershop stuff. It'll be great."

I saw the logic of his idea, but I knew that it could not raise money if there wasn't any. "But Buster, nobody has any money to pay to get into a show. Everybody's broke because of the depression."

Buster was always thinking. "Well, no matter how much money you got, you can't eat it. So we're gonna get people to bring food for admission. The price of admission is a jar of preserves, a cantaloupe, a pumpkin, fish—whatever people can eat. I know it's late in the year, but everybody's got an extra jar of canned peaches or apples. That's all we'll ask. Just one of anything."

Say what you want about Buster's impish tendencies, he stayed on the right track for this one. The school gym would be free, the performers would be free ,and the food that we collected would be given to the hungry. If I didn't know how the story ended up, I would ask, *What could go wrong?*

Mr. Bevel, the school principle, gave us permission to use the gym for the show in two weeks. Buster enlisted as many of kids as he could to make signs, perform, and spread the word. Buster got Rosie to ask her father to be the host of ceremonies. Without knowing that Buster was behind the whole idea, he agreed.

We were all surprised at how much talent lived in our little town. Singers, dancers, violinists, pianists, and banjo players. There were fourteen acts and a short skit written by Buster. Again, the mayor had not been aware of Buster's involvement.

We were still in a recession. The bank stayed busy with foreclosures, collections, and very selective lending. Even after the mayor knew that Rosie would be taking a starring role in the play, he failed to ask who else was involved.

The butcher donated paper for the signs. The date, time, and cost of entry was posted over many parts of the city.

In late September, not much else was going on in our little town. The show was announced in all three churches. It was mentioned on the radio, and the newspaper ran a free ad. Buster's idea had grown into a full-fledged program.

Buster's skit involved three people: Buster, Rosie and me. I would be her first customer at a bake sale. After paying, my role was finished. My two short lines were simple to remember.

Buster and Rosie were the stars of the skit. It centered on a special person who approaches the bake sale vendor and asks her what she is planning to do with the money from the sale. She explains that it is going to be used to buy new hymnals for the church. Buster buys a cookie but uses very rare and valuable money for the purchase.

The money turns out to be a small fortune. At the end of the play, Rosie's character says she will use some of the money to help people in the town save their houses. Then she gives Buster a kiss. A sweet enough play—if it did not target the mayor for being the one to take people's houses. And, of course, his daughter was to be kissed by his nemesis.

The mayor fumed while he watched the play and seemed glad when it finished. At the end of the show, he had been given a list of participants to thank for raising several bags of food for the hungry.

Mr. Bevel handed the Mayor the list. He began reading the names of the participants and donors. When he neared the end of the list, he prepared to introduce the producer and director of the play. He started thanking the genius behind the production until his eyes fell to the name. It became evident that he was trying not to become angry in front of the large audience.

He quickly announced that the whole ordeal owed its thanks to Buster. Then he crumpled the list and walked off the stage as Buster took a bow.

The pantry at the gas station had enough food to help many travelers. This started the first food bank in the town, ensuring people could at least last another few days because of the kindness of the locals.

The picture on the front page of the paper the next day showed Rosie kissing Buster with a mass of food behind them. The mayor could not be found for comment.

7

One day during the summer between our junior and senior year of high school, we were on our way to the swimming hole. Of course, we had to make our usual dash across the pasture. This time, however, Ol' Snort almost got us. We reached the oak tree just in time.

"Whew, that was close," said Buster. "I felt his horns on the bottom of my shoes as I climbed the tree."

Instead of splashing in the swimming hole, we sat in the tree for nearly three hours. It was over one-hundred degrees that day. For hours the bull leisurely ate the shady grass below us. Any attempt to get out of the tree would have resulted in being gored, trampled, and left for dead. This bull was keen on two things besides eating: mating with the cows and trying to eliminate the kids that cut through the pasture.

We accepted this bull as a threat to our lives. Looking back as an adult, it seems strange that we did. This bull was intent on killing us. And we just dealt with him as if he was a part of the landscape.

The bull finally moved far enough away for us to run back to the gate. Our swimming hole activities were cancelled. Ol' Snort gave chase but wasn't as speedy as before. Maybe the heat affected him too.

Buster, angry about wasting a day to swim, vowed revenge. I accepted the situation with more grace than Buster did. To be honest, I always felt relieved when I lived through the run for the back fence.

Buster's father had a pellet rifle that he kept in the back of the house. He used it to keep the foxes from bothering the hens. It could pump up to .22 caliber strength. Both Buster and I had taken the gun a few times for shooting expeditions. We weren't supposed to use it without Lafayette around, but that never stopped us.

Buster hurried home and grabbed the pellet rifle.

Shoving it down his pant leg, he walked stiff-legged until he was beyond sight of his home. Then he pulled out the rifle, pumping it as he walked. He reached maximum power as he got to the gate at Miller's pasture. Ol' Snort stood halfway between the gate and the oak tree. He paid little attention to the boy with the pellet gun.

In Buster's defense, I knew he had always been kind to animals. So he aimed at the bull's rear. He only wanted to give the bull a little discomfort, as the bull had done to us for most of the afternoon.

"I just want you to have a sore rear like I do. You kept me in that tree for three hours, Snort," Buster grumbled.

As Buster squeezed the trigger, the bull moved. Instead of getting shot in the rear, the pellet hit the bull's scrotum. His heard jerked up, eyes wide. He started running like crazy. A sound came out of his mouth like a low train whistle.

The bull ran right through the north fence, ending up in farmer Miller's barn yard. Mrs. Miller ran from the coop area, dropping the eggs she'd been collecting. The two Miller kids barely made it inside the barn before the bull charged them. Mr. Miller was working in the tool shed when he saw the mad bull attack his family.

"Everybody stay where they are," yelled the farmer.

"He's gone mad. He'll kill one of us if he can."

The farmer grabbed his hunting rifle. As the bull ran toward the shed, the farmer shot him between the eyes. The bull stopped three feet short of the farmer and fell to one side.

The Miller's gave bull meat to all their neighbors. It turned out that the bull was past his breeding prime. The farmer planned to shoot and butcher the bull soon anyway. Buster had only hurried the demise of his enemy.

Buster felt very bad about the incident. But I was the only one he ever told what really happened that day.

I felt a little funny when Julia Miller, the farmer's daughter, brought us a piece of bull steak. But I knew that if I had ever stumbled while being chased by Ol' Snort, it would have been my misfortune before his.

Fittingly, they gave Buster's family a rump roast…

Buster put the rifle back without being detected. The Millers never figured out why their bull had gone berserk. Their new bull appeared very shy. He took little notice when we ran through the pasture.

We called the replacement bull Ferdinand.

8

The same summer as the demise of Ol' Snort, Buster decided he needed to make money.

The depression had a tight financial grip on us all. Companies did not have enough money to hire workers. Jobs in the city were already over-filled. Layoffs were all too common. Buster's father tried to find something on the railroad for him, but new hires were rare.

"You know..." There was that phrase again. "I'll bet I could use my bike and deliver stuff around town. Like the kids do in New York City!"

I didn't point out the problem with comparing a clustered, heavily populated city like New York to a spread-out farming community like ours.

Buster rubbed the seat of his bike. It had parts from every bicycle manufactured at the time. Stubby Minkle at the machine shop even welded on the frame to make it last. It was a present for Buster when he turned eleven. The innertubes were a series of many patches. The inside of the rubber tires had spots where Buster had glued the rubber shut to prevent holes.

Most kids those days repaired their own bicycles. Buster had become a very resourceful repairmen, even if some of the parts came from baby carriages, tricycles, chain saws, and pumps.

Buster visited the businesses in town that needed a delivery man. He ended up convincing the drug store, the grocery store, Doc Floog, O'Grady's butcher shop, and Miller's dairy to consider his service. Gas for automobiles had become difficult to acquire. To Buster's credit, it seemed cost-effective for a kid to take a prescription on his bike across town rather than driving it out.

Buster began his delivery business right away. He completed three deliveries the first week. He was paid by the businesses and tipped by the people receiving the items. The tips were usually in the form of a cold drink or something to eat, but hey—he had a business.

After the third week, Buster was doing a couple deliveries per day. Some were as far as nine miles outside of the city. He made the deliveries regardless of how far they were.

His plan was going well until the pharmacy gave him a bag to deliver to Hopkins farm. It was about six miles outside of town. Karl Hopkins, a local pig farmer, had a sow that needed laxatives. The pills the pharmacy provided were strengthened for livestock.

Karl's wife, Betty, had been under a doctor's care for weight loss. She had started taking amphetamines to control her appetite. Using diet pills for obesity was popular in the 1930s. Few people in the town knew of Betty's efforts to decrease her girth.

Buster felt it was good luck that he could deliver Betty's pills and the pig's pills on the same day.

Buster picked up the bag of laxatives and amphetamines around two in the afternoon. Then he peddled out to Hopkins farm. The day was unusually hot. When he reached the four-mile mark, he stopped at a bridge over the creek. The cool water remained too attractive for him to ignore. In only his underwear, Buster sat in the cool creek water and enjoyed the shade under the bridge. The bags were still on the back of his bike.

Unfortunately, the dogs from Miller's dairy, Blue and Yeller, found the bike while Buster soaked. The chocolaty covering on the laxative was too hard for Blue to resist. For unknown reasons, Yeller devoured the colorful diet pills. They scampered home before Buster returned.

When Buster saw the damage to his packages, he had no choice but to return to the pharmacy. Everyone assumed a local raccoon had raided the delivery.

Meanwhile, Mrs. Miller called the hounds in for dinner. She put down bowls of food down for them. Then she returned to the kitchen to bake a pie.

Over the normal, savory smells of the kitchen, a terrible odor wafted through the house. Julia, the Miller's daughter, smelled and then saw a terrible sight in the living room. The throw rugs were covered with dog excrement from the pig laxatives. Both hounds looked quite unwell. Blue was evacuating his bowels. Yeller, stimulated by the amphetamines, ran in circles around the room, over the sofa, back to front door, halfway up the stairs, and so on.

Julia screamed and let Yeller outside. He ran through town at the speed of light. No one tried to stop the hound as it broke speed laws downtown. Yeller was found three days later thirty miles away, asleep on a hay stack.

Blue was tossed outside. He only went as far as the barnyard before instinct took over and he began eating clay.

When the Miller's called the vet, he put two-and-two together. The vet figured out where the pills destined for the Hopkins farm had ended up.

Buster worked for free for a week to make up for the loss to the pharmacy. The Miller's blamed Buster as well, but there were two sides to that story.

Mrs. Miller went to visit her sister in Akron. Julia went to see her grandmother in Detroit. Mr. Miller stayed in the barn until the strong scent of cleaner, used to get rid of Blue's mess inside the house, was gone.

When the house was fresh again, the Millers built a dog house for the hounds. They all agreed to never let them inside again. Both dogs took a while to put weight back on.

Buster

9

Buster became an impressive senior at our high school. He was member of the football team, he joined the band, and he became editor of the school newspaper. He was popular with the kids, as well as some of the teachers. But he was still the mayor's nemesis.

This really presented a problem for Buster. You see, he started dating Rosie. But they had to keep it on the sly. Normal dates were covered with her attending functions by herself or with a girlfriend and then spending the evening with Buster. But prom season was its own beast.

Prom had customs. For example, the girl's date picks her up at her house. She's given a corsage, and the parents take pictures of the young couple. This would be impossible for Buster and Rosie. Her father would have had a heart attack if he knew she was going to prom with Buster.

Buster finally came to me and said, "You know... We could pretend to take each other's girlfriend to prom. Then we can switch dates at the gym. I don't think Rosie's dad hates you like he hates me."

I couldn't refuse the request after the favors he had done for me over the years. I agreed and the girls did too. Rosie made sure her father only a mildly disliked of me.

"Isn't he a friend of that Buster kid?" the mayor grumbled to Rosie. Rosie assured him that Buster and I had grown apart during high school and rarely spoke. The kids in the school knew the two of us were inseparable, but that information was kept within the student body.

None of us had a car. Luckily, my real date's father, Mr. Chingall, had a six-year old model A. It ran quite well. He agreed to chauffeur us to the prom and back. Buster and I each chipped in a dime for gas.

Both Buster and I did extra chores so we could come up with enough money to get a corsage from the florist.

The cost for a corsage was over one dollar. Even at that price there were not any inexpensive flowers used in our little town. I had to save every penny I made. I even borrowed a quarter from my folks to afford the corsage for Becky.

Buster had to give it to Becky at her house. I had to give Rosie her corsage at the mayor's home. It was an easy plan that should never have gone wrong.

Mr. Chingall picked up the boys first so we could pull up to the girl's homes and escort our dates to the car. He went back to his own house so Buster could go in and get Becky. Becky secretly had a crush on Buster so this worked out better for her than normally would be expected. They returned to the car and we were off to pick up Rosie.

I had not been in the Mayor's house since Rosie's twelfth birthday party. It made me a little anxious to go into the house. I knew the mayor was not fond of any of the local boys when it came to his daughter.

Buster remained in the car. He stayed as low as possible to remain undetected in case the mayor looked out to the car.

Mrs. Traufman fussed over our appearances as well-dressed young people. She complimented the corsage as I fitted it to Rosie's wrist. Rosie thanked me dutifully. Within moments we were ready to leave. Thankfully the mayor did not walk us out to the car.

"Remember, home by twelve," the mayor reminded me. He gave my shoulder a painful squeeze on my way out. This created a fear in me. I thought about the fact that he ran the police department and held the mortgage on my parent's house. I began to be worry about what Buster had gotten me into.

After getting out of the car and walking to the gymnasium, we looked back to make sure Mr. Chingall had left. When we were sure he was gone, we switched dates.

We entered the dance and felt very proud of our accomplishment. The feeling lasted most of the evening as we enjoyed the dance. The local band played top hits from the 20s and 30s. Everything worked out fine until the coronation.

One aspect we had not considered in our elaborate scam was when the ballots were read. Buster and Rosie were crowned as king and queen of the prom. That might have been ok, except for the picture.

The photographer for the local paper snapped a picture of prom king and queen for the front page. The four of us knew there would be hell to pay the next day. It was hard for Rosie to even smile. Buster had that lost look

I'd seen a couple of years before in the telephone booth. Their dance that followed was both touching and ominous.

As planned, Becky called her father around 10 PM. She told him that one of the other kids had a large car and would give all of us a ride home. That way, he wouldn't have to pick us up. He was reluctant at first. But Becky was eighteen. And for some reason, he felt he could trust her with Buster. Our plan was to walk home so we could spend some special time together without the prying eyes of parents.

Outside the gym, we talked about how bad it was going to be for Rosie once her father read the newspaper. We strolled the couple of miles to our neighborhood. We would have been home early enough if we had not stopped by the park. Each couple found a bench, far apart from the other.

Buster and Rosie went over by the stream that ran through the back of the park. They sat under an old elm tree. When the rain came, all four of us ran for the awning over the pharmacy. It took an hour for the rain to let up enough to walk the girls home.

It was 1:30 by the time I walked Rosie to her door. I shook her hand and thanked her for a wonderful evening. The Mayor turned on the porch light, walked out, and ordered her to her room.

He was a stout man over sixty. He was not pleased. He chased me off his yard and nearly caught sight of Buster as I ran for the street. I knew it was useless to explain what had happened.

Becky's father was also angry. He slammed the front door shut as Buster walked away. We talked a little on our way home and decided that joining the Air Force was probably our best option. Our plan was to pack and be out by the time the paper hit the mayor's house. We were guilty on so many levels. There was no way out.

My parents woke me in the morning but were not too upset. Dad said the mayor had called him and complained about us getting home so late. I told my father we had arranged a ride but it fell through. Then we were caught in the rain.

That explanation would have been okay—until the newspaper circulated. Dad never liked the mayor much. I think he would have been happy if I had dated Rosie. But that picture provide we all had lied about our prom dates.

Rosie was sent east to live with her Aunt while the mess was sorted out. She and Buster did not see each other again for over twenty years. Buster's parents were not too upset. They understood that the mayor had a thing against Buster.

Becky's father finally became understanding of the incident. Ultimately, it was only the mayor that remained upset. He may have gotten over it if the picture of Buster and Rosie had not been put in the front window of the Daily Monitor headquarters. There it was displayed for everyone to enjoy.

The person who broke the front window of the Daily Monitor is still unknown. However, the mayor's name was mentioned several times.

Buster

10

Graduation went smoothly for most of us. Buster showed his normal big grin as he walked across the gym floor and was handed his diploma by Mrs. Oates.

As graduates, we had the customary party that night at Bradshaw's barn. Somebody spiked the punch so the party was even louder than usual. Most of us knew we may not see each other again. Rumors of some guy name Hitler in Europe made all of us uneasy for our future. Buster was no exception.

Buster's father allowed him to use his 1932 Buick

that night. This was a huge surprise. Buster's father treasured that car. He spent hours keeping it shined up and gleaming. He had been known to stop during trips to clean off bugs from the grill or to chase birds after they dropped a surprise on the roof.

Any stop downtown resulted in him bringing out a rag and cleaning off the road dust on the chrome.

Of course, the mayor had a better car: a 1935 Road Master. Buster looked very impressive driving to Bradshaw's. I enjoyed sitting up front, overlooking the long black hood. We had spent hours that day cleaning the car for this trip.

It was June, so Buster parked under the big elm by the barn to keep the car cool. We spent all evening at the good-bye party. When we returned to the car, even in the dark, we realized our mistake. In the hot weather, the hens his in this tree for shade. There was little black to be seen on the Buick's horizontal surfaces—it was covered in chicken poop! We knew Buster's father would be livid.

"My dad's not gonna be happy about this," said Buster. "I gotta clean this up before he sees it tomorrow morning."

I thought for a moment and said, "How 'bout the river? We could drive to the shallow crossing part and clean the bird drops off with the water."

"Good idea."

Buster put the car into gear, and we rolled toward the creek.

We parked the car in the shallow creek. The water came up to the running boards. We splashed water onto the roof and hood to get the hen crap loose from the paint.

The plan was working until Buster said, "You know... I think we could do better if we got the bucket from the trunk and poured water over the top. I'll get it out. You climb up on the roof. Careful not to leave any footprints up there."

It might have been a good idea, but we were working with water in pitch darkness.

Buster filled several buckets full of water before we decided the car was clean enough. After a little trouble unsticking the car from the riverbed, drove on home. I spent the night at Buster's in his spare bedroom. I was satisfied that we had avoided the problem of the hens.

"What the hell have you done to my car?" Lafayette screamed up at Buster's window the next morning. "Dammit you guys. What did you do to it?"

We both jumped out of bed and looked down at the

car. It was now a tan color from all the mud in the river water. It had dried over the entire car. To make it worse, small minnows had spent the night dying in seams and joints around the body of the car.

We dressed quickly and ran outside. It not only looked awful, but the dead fish odor was horrible. Both of us stood with our mouths agape as we tried to figure out a way to explain what had happened.

We spent four hours cleaning the car. Buster's father sat in a chair under the tree in the front of the house. His eyes never left us.

The next day, a Monday, Buster signed up for the Air Force. I mailed my application over to Michigan State University. We spent the rest of the day peeling potatoes for Buster's mother.

Buster left three days later amid hugs and well-wishes. Frances saw her son off. The rest of us realized that when Buster left, an era in our town come to an end.

We were not ones to write. I only heard third-hand about Buster's exploits in the military, but it is my understanding that Selfridge Air Force Base had many unexplained activities. To me, it seemed like they all pointed to Buster.

The day after Buster left, the mayor drove his new

Buick down Main Street before it stalled. The mayor had the car towed to Dahlgood's repair and found out that somebody had crammed a potato up his tailpipe.

The mayor began walking to his office after leaving his car to be repaired. As he passed by the tree with his name on it, the one he had planted on Arbor Day many years before, he saw a sign that said "Pee on Me." It was hung on the lower branches.

I had to agree, it did look like Buster's penmanship.

About The Author

Darryl Armstong is a contributing author to the Storyshares library.

About The Publisher

Story Shares is a nonprofit focused on supporting the millions of teens and adults who struggle with reading by creating a new shelf in the library specifically for them. The ever-growing collection features content that is compelling and culturally relevant for teens and adults, yet still readable at a range of lower reading levels.

Story Shares generates content by engaging deeply with writers, bringing together a community to create this new kind of book. With more intriguing and approachable stories to choose from, the teens and adults who have fallen behind are improving their skills and beginning to discover the joy of reading. For more information, visit storyshares.org.

Easy to Read. Hard to Put Down.

Buster

www.ingramcontent.com/pod-product-compliance
Lightning Source LLC
Chambersburg PA
CBHW071223170626
46809CB00005BA/1910